M000158672

The Fairytale Lives of Russian Girls
(or, *девушки*)

Meg Miroshnik

A Samuel French Acting Edition

FOUNDED 1830

SAMUELFRENCH.COM
SAMUELFRENCH-LONDON.CO.UK

Copyright © 2014 by Meg Miroshnik
All Rights Reserved

THE FAIRYTALE LIVES OF RUSSIAN GIRLS is fully protected under the copyright laws of the United States of America, the British Commonwealth, including Canada, and all other countries of the Copyright Union. All rights, including professional and amateur stage productions, recitation, lecturing, public reading, motion picture, radio broadcasting, television and the rights of translation into foreign languages are strictly reserved.

ISBN 978-0-573-70364-5

www.SamuelFrench.com
www.SamuelFrench-London.co.uk

FOR PRODUCTION ENQUIRIES

UNITED STATES AND CANADA
Info@SamuelFrench.com
1-866-598-8449

UNITED KINGDOM AND EUROPE
Plays@SamuelFrench-London.co.uk
020-7255-4302

Each title is subject to availability from Samuel French, depending upon country of performance. Please be aware that *THE FAIRYTALE LIVES OF RUSSIAN GIRLS* may not be licensed by Samuel French in your territory. Professional and amateur producers should contact the nearest Samuel French office or licensing partner to verify availability.

CAUTION: Professional and amateur producers are hereby warned that *THE FAIRYTALE LIVES OF RUSSIAN GIRLS* is subject to a licensing fee. Publication of this play(s) does not imply availability for performance. Both amateurs and professionals considering a production are strongly advised to apply to Samuel French before starting rehearsals, advertising, or booking a theatre. A licensing fee must be paid whether the title(s) is presented for charity or gain and whether or not admission is charged. Professional/Stock licensing fees are quoted upon application to Samuel French.

No one shall make any changes in this title(s) for the purpose of production. No part of this book may be reproduced, stored in a retrieval system, or transmitted in any form, by any means, now known or yet to be invented, including mechanical, electronic, photocopying, recording, videotaping, or otherwise, without the prior written permission of the publisher. No one shall upload this title(s), or part of this title(s), to any social media websites.

For all enquiries regarding motion picture, television, and other media rights, please contact Samuel French.

MUSIC USE NOTE

Licensees are solely responsible for obtaining formal written permission from copyright owners to use copyrighted music in the performance of this play and are strongly cautioned to do so. If no such permission is obtained by the licensee, then the licensee must use only original music that the licensee owns and controls. Licensees are solely responsible and liable for all music clearances and shall indemnify the copyright owners of the play(s) and their licensing agent, Samuel French, against any costs, expenses, losses and liabilities arising from the use of music by licensees. Please contact the appropriate music licensing authority in your territory for the rights to any incidental music.

IMPORTANT BILLING AND CREDIT REQUIREMENTS

If you have obtained performance rights to this title, please refer to your licensing agreement for important billing and credit requirements.

THE FAIRYTALE LIVES OF RUSSIAN GIRLS is the winner of the 2011–2012 Alliance/Kendeda Graduate Playwriting Award and was first produced by the Alliance Theatre in February 2012 (Artistic Director, Susan V. Booth). The production was directed by Eric Rosen.

THE FAIRYTALE LIVES OF RUSSIAN GIRLS was subsequently produced by the Yale Repertory Theatre (James Bundy, Artistic Director; Victoria Nolan, Managing Director) in New Haven, Connecticut. The opening date was February 6, 2014. The performance was directed by Rachel Chavkin, with sets by Christopher Ash, costumes by KJ Kim, lighting by Bradley King, and sound design, music direction, and original music by Chad Raines. The Production Stage Manager was Hannah Sullivan. The cast was as follows:

ANNIE	Emily Walton
MASHA	Sofiya Akilova
KATYA	Celeste Arias
OTHER KATYA/NASTYA	Stéphanie Hayes
OLGA/PASSPORT CONTROL OFFICER/	
PROFESSOR/VALENTINA	Jessica Jelliffe
BABA YAGA/YAROSLAVA	Felicity Jones

CHARACTERS

ANNIE – 20, the American

MASHA – 19, the Girlfriend

KATYA – 19, the Mistress

One actress plays:

THE OTHER KATYA, 19, the Daughter/NASTYA, 20, the Whore

One actress, 40s, plays:

OLGA/PASSPORT CONTROL OFFICER/PROFESSOR/VALENTINA

One actress, older, plays:

BABA YAGA/AUNTIE YAROSLAVA

SETTING

Moscow 2005: the thrice-nine tsardom in the thrice-ten country.

AUTHOR'S NOTES

Olga is the only character who speaks with an accent; everyone else is communicating in their native language. Transliterations of Russian words into English don't always correspond with the Library of Congress's Romanization system.

For Stan

1. "Masha and the Bear."

(**MASHA**, *19, is getting dressed to go out. She zips up thigh-high fire-engine red boots and plays with long, thin cigarettes from a pack labeled "Vogue".*)

MASHA. *Zhili byli.*

In Russian means:

They lived, they were.

Once upon a time.

Start your stories with it,

spin your *skazki* on it.

Zhili byli.

They lived, they were:

a mother and her daughter in a one-room shack on the edge of the forest.

The father?

I think he got killed in a hit-and-run when he stepped off the breadcrumb path.

(This was very sad, of course.

But it also meant that the toilet seat was never left up again.)

Now, the daughter, Masha...

(gestures to self:)

(Menya zavut Masha)

was, of course, always dreaming about running away into the forest.

'Cuz that's where everything good –

meaning everything bad –

happened.

But shitty as her mother's little shack was, Masha was afraid to go out on her own.

Until, one day, two boys came by wondering if she could come out and play.

Now, Masha REALLY WANTED to come out and play.

She asked her mother;

Mozhno pozhalusta hodit v les?

So I can, uh…gather mushrooms and berries to feed to you, Mama?

And Masha's mother said: *Mozhno.*

They'd been sharing a single room for a really fricking long time and Mama had some personal

things she'd like to attend to with some amount of privacy, too, y'know?

So, Mama said: *Mozhno*, but remember, Masha, to stick to the –

Masha was gone and off the path before the words came out of her mother's mouth.

She went deep in to the forest where those boys showed her how to:

Thrust into the earth to dig up mushrooms and part bushes to gobble up juicy berries…

Omigod.

These were the kind of chores Masha could get used to!

After a few hours of hard work, the sky darkened and the boys stole away.

Said they were going on a "beer run".

And Masha was left alone in the forest where everything good –

Meaning everything bad –

Happens.

After dark. Off the path. Out of luck.

When Masha came upon a hut.

Actually not so much a hut as a cottage.

Hell, compared to the one-room shack? A palace.

With a cozy fire.

A pie cooling on the window sill.

(The best part:)

And it was empty.

So, Masha went inside and made herself at home.

*(**MASHA** takes off her shirt and lounges in her red bra: The fantasy of what women do when they are alone. A huge, hairy **FIGURE** appears in silhouette.)*

But all houses have masters.

And the *hozain* of this hut came home.

*(The **FIGURE** takes a few heavy steps toward her, threateningly. It looms over **MASHA**, but she makes all the noises.)*

It sounded something like: Grrrrrrrrrllllllllll.

Masha couldn't see anything, so she said: Grrrrl?

Grrrrrrrrrrrrrrrrrrllllllllllllllllll.

And Masha said: Girl?

GIRL.

*(**MASHA** turns to see the **FIGURE** towering over her.)*

DYE-VU-SHKA!

(Which means grrrrlll *pa russky*.)

Grrrrrl, what are you doing in my house?

I didn't know this house belonged to a bear!

Believe me, if I'd known a *medved* lived here –

It was just – it was after dark and I was alone and your house was so cozy and your bed looked just right –

Please! Are you going to eat me up?

Are you going to put your paws all over my body?

Run your claws through my soft flesh?

Are you going to shred me into strips and chew on the strings of me for hours?

(A beat.)

The bear thought for a moment.

*(The **FIGURE** gets in her face.)*

And the *medved* said to Masha.

No, *dyevushka*, I will not eat you.

I will keep you

in my hut.

You will stoke my stove.

You will cook my kasha porridge.

You will feed me my kasha porridge.

I will never, ever let you go.

'Til death do us part.

(The FIGURE *grabs her.* MASHA *looks at the FIGURE, disappointed.)*

Oh, god, Masha said.

A lifetime commitment?

Is your mind 100% made up?

I mean, are you sure you wouldn't rather just eat me?

(Lights shift. The FIGURE *is now completely visible. It is* ANNIE, *20, a small girl in an enormous old and mangy hooded fur coat. She removes the hood before speaking.)*

ANNIE. Don't worry, I'm not a fuckwit.

I know fur is totally murder.

Blackmail was involved in making me wear it.

It's so ancient – my mom had it before she had me.

OLGA. Hhhhhhoney.

2. "The sun'll come up. Tomorrow."

*(Enter **OLGA**, 42, **ANNIE**'s mother. She wears a pastel velour tracksuit and has spray-tanned skin and highlighted hair.)*

ANNIE. Mo-om, it's so ugly and huge. I can't wear it.

OLGA. Hhhhhoney, you haf to understand. It's dark ages when I receive zis. Literally. In Soviet Union, KGB turns on sun only one hour each day. Zey had switch. One coat – it needed last you whole life: Pregnancy, fattening up, becoming old, stooping woman. One coat you haf to wear true all of it.

ANNIE. But, Ma, it's June. I'm only gonna be in Moscow until August.

OLGA. When I am young, I see dead people standing in streets – it's so cold zey freeze standing up to ground. And zis is July. You need fur, Annie. And you need zis.

*(**OLGA** removes a safety pin from inside her tracksuit and pins it to the fur.)*

ANNIE. Oh my god, an evil eye?

OLGA. You *father* evil eye. To ward off danger.

ANNIE. Ma, I don't believe in evil eyes –

OLGA. He cannot be killed, you father Koschei the Deathless, because he is demon who has hidden soul separate from body.

ANNIE. C'mon, Mom. Dad moved to Tennessee with his second family.

OLGA. When he spirit away! You Russian go like rust. You lose words, you get accent.

ANNIE. I started calling myself Annie like the orphan.

OLGA. Now, you learn grown-up Russian, business vocabulary. You not little *dyevochka* any more.

ANNIE. You're the one who's always calling me a *dyevushka*.

OLGA. Completely different thing. *Dyevochka* is little girl. *Dyevushka* is girl under age of seventy.

ANNIE. I took women's studies. That's like, offensive. Females over eighteen are women.

OLGA. Baby, in Russia, you girl until you senior citizen. Consolation for hard life zere.

ANNIE. If it's so effing hard, why do I have to go?

OLGA. I come here for you – you sink zis effing easy?

ANNIE. We got religious asylum.

OLGA. This was gonna be country of happily ever after. Not country of all day on feet washing stranger hair. Now, I see on TV, all zees Russian people (not Jewish) who stay has so much mahnies. Zey get free apartments from Soviet government, zen capitalist real estate market goes crazy and everybody gets so rich, zey cover all toilets in gold and use mahnies to vipe they asses.

ANNIE. What does any of this have to do with me?

OLGA. You *dyevushka* in *skazka* who return home to Rus to reap you rewards. You gotta take you legacy, baby.

ANNIE. Then why don't *you* return home to Rus? Doesn't bad shit happen to girls who get sent into the forest?

OLGA. I'm too old. Plus, I never knew how to ask no questions.

ANNIE. What?

OLGA. Exactly. You haf address?

ANNIE. In my pocket.

OLGA. You not-really-Auntie Yaroslava place was just like *you very own home* –

ANNIE. My *not-really Aunt?*

OLGA. We not really blood.

She's not Jewish.

But you make her treat you good, baby.

ANNIE. Am I seriously going?

OLGA. I see you in *Avgust.*

ANNIE. I guess.

(They hug.)

If I don't *die* first.

OLGA. What?

ANNIE. From, like, the heat exhaustion of wearing a family of beavers on my back.

(ANNIE *starts to exit.*)

OLGA. Annie, wait!

I need show you –

(OLGA *starts to unzip her tracksuit jacket.*)

ANNIE. Eew, Mom, keep your clothes on!

(OLGA *grabs* ANNIE *by the wrist to stop her from going. She puts* ANNIE*'s hand on a scar on her chest.*)

What – ? Where did you get that scar?

OLGA. Russia.

(ANNIE *looks.*)

ANNIE. Mom, it's shaped like the Soviet Union.

(OLGA *zips up her jacket quickly.*)

OLGA. Watch out for witches. Wicked witches is crazy bitches.

ANNIE. Wait, *what?*

OLGA. Sleep wis one eye open, baby.

(OLGA *disappears.* ANNIE *sets off, unsteadily.*)

ANNIE. Once upon a time, a woman who was a girl who would always be a *dyevushka*, set out on a journey.

(*A rush of sound as* ANNIE *exits and the light shift and we are suddenly in Moscow, the thrice-nine tsardom in the thrice-ten country.*)

3. "Baba Yaga with the Bony Leg."

(**BABA YAGA/YAROSLAVA** *shuffles onstage.*)

BABA YAGA. Baba Yaga did not want to be disturbed,
so she found a hut far away from the tourist center.
Anything you have ever seen in a picture –
Red Square? Or the Kremlin? –
is located far away from the realm of Baba Yaga. in the land of the Truly Dead.
Baba Yaga did not want to be surprised,
so she set that hut atop tall chicken legs
that run in wild circles if a stranger ever approaches.
The hut also lets out blood-curdling screams,
so that no one may ever sneak up on Baba Yaga,
especially little girls (those sneaky little bitches).
Baba Yaga did not want to be bothered,
so she surrounded the hut with a fence made of bones.
Each bone post is topped by a skull with eye sockets that glow like coals in the dark.
Oh, did Baba Yaga mention? There is one empty bone post.
In case a pretty little skull should happen her way.
To do her bidding and keep her company, Baba Yaga has enchanted three flying hands.
But do not ask about them.
In fact, do not ask about anything.
For every time Baba Yaga is asked a question…
She ages one year!
This is one of the reasons she despises little girls.
They always ask questions:
Why do you look so old, Baba Yaga?
Why do you have such bony legs, Baba Yaga?
Why are you so mean, do you hate me,
Why do you hate me, Baba Yaga?

And just like that, little girl, in five seconds, Baba Yaga
has aged five years.

(**BABA YAGA**'s *face becomes even more pinched.*)

This is why she feels three hundred and three.
And she does not like it one bit.

(*She feels her face, assessing the damage.*)

But there are some things Baba Yaga does like:
Big bowls of borsch that have chunks of fatty beef in
every bite,
giant dumplings stuffed with cheese and potatoes,
and hot loaves of bread fresh from her big brick oven.
You see, she may look like one of those brittle *babushki*
begging on the Moscow metro,
but every night, Baba Yaga eats a meal large enough to
feed four soldiers.
Yet she is never full.
She has never been satisfied.
And with her mouth full of jagged iron teeth,
there is *nothing* Baba Yaga can't eat.

(**YAROSLAVA** *settles into a chair to sleep in a shadowy
corner, one eye open and trained on the audience.*)

4. "Annie at the Airport."

(The stage swirls with movement and sound as **ANNIE** *enters.)*

OFFICER. *(unseen) Dyevushka!*

(The stage suddenly parts to reveal the **PASSPORT CONTROL OFFICER**, *a domineering figure in the Victoria's Secret version of border-control apparel.)*

Passport, please.

Dyevushka!

*(***ANNIE** *pulls her passport out of the fur.)*

Amerikanka.

*(***OFFICER** *opens up the passport.)*

...named *Anya Rabinovich.*

ANNIE. Annie, like the orphan.

OFFICER. Born Moscow.

ANNIE. I was a little Soviet citizen.

OFFICER. A tiny baby Jew.

ANNIE. Oh, yeah, I guess.

OFFICER. And now you are back.

ANNIE. Three-month student visa. I've returned home to Rus to reap my rewards.

(The **OFFICER** *looks up at her sharply.)*

OFFICER. Then you should have a *skazochnaya* visa, not a student one.

ANNIE. Ha. A fairytale visa.

(beat)

You're serious?

OFFICER. Where are you living, foreign girl?

ANNIE. The address is on my migration card.

(The **OFFICER** *looks at the card, then she looks back at the shadowy corner where* **YAROSLAVA** *sleeps.)*

OFFICER. This is on the other side of the River of Fire.

ANNIE. The what – ?

OFFICER. Once you leave the land of the Truly Dead...
There's nothing your embassy will be able to do for you, *dyevushka*.

You sure you want to make this trip?

ANNIE. Yes?

*(The **OFFICER** stamps the passport with finality.)*

OFFICER. *Dobra pozhaluvat.* A very friendly welcome to Russia.

*(Another swirl of activity and sound as **ANNIE** walks toward **YAROSLAVA**.)*

ANNIE. *(again, unsteadily)* Something is not right here. I haven't believed in *skazki* since the Soviet Union, but still –

When a *dyevushka* is pushed from home to a land far, far away...

*(**ANNIE** consults a scrap of paper.)*

Building 99, Tower 7, Entrance 3, Apartment Number 57.

*(**ANNIE** looks up.)*

She should keep her wits about her.

*(**ANNIE** refers back to the paper, then looks up.)*

Building 99.

*(**ANNIE** takes a step toward the building.)*

Something is not right here.

It looks foreign...but familiar?

Tower number 7.

Like my very own home.

*(**ANNIE** sees a figure in a hooded red sweatshirt **MASHA** step into the shadows.)*

Hey!

(**ANNIE** *looks up at the door.*)

Entrance number 3.

(**ANNIE** *opens the door.*)

Sleep with one eye open.

5. "Auntie Yaroslava's Apartment."

(**ANNIE** *looks at the door.*)

ANNIE. Hello?

(**YAROSLAVA** *cringes: Every time she's asked a question, she ages one year.*)

Anyone here?

(*Another cringe.* **ANNIE** *reaches for the door handle hesitantly; it swings open at the lightest touch and* **ANNIE** *enters the apartment.*)

Oh, ew. Gold toilets my ass.

(**ANNIE** *sees the sleeping* **YAROSLAVA**.)

Hello?

(*She reaches out to gently nudge* **YAROSLAVA**, *who suddenly bolts upright and snaps at* **ANNIE**'s *hand. She misses, but her iron teeth make a loud metallic sound.*)

Oh, SHIT!

YAROSLAVA. *Dyevushka!*

ANNIE. Yaroslava Yanovna, it's me: Anya Rabinovich.

YAROSLAVA. What?

ANNIE. My mom told you I was coming?

YAROSLAVA. Who?

ANNIE. My mom, Olga Rabinovich.

YAROSLAVA. Ah, yes. Olga, Olga, Olga.

ANNIE. She *did* tell you I was coming?

YAROSLAVA. Oh, yes, dearie. I had forgotten that today was the special day. How is your mother?

ANNIE. Okay, I guess. She stopped being a mathematician when we moved to America. Now she works as a hairdresser in a fancy salon.

YAROSLAVA. And your father...

ANNIE. He left us, oh, I don't know, ten years ago.

YAROSLAVA. An orphan.

ANNIE. I'm not an orphan. That's when your parents are dead. Both my parents are still alive.

YAROSLAVA. Oh, dear. My apologies.

ANNIE. How do you know my mom again?

(YAROSLAVA *winces at the question.*)

YAROSLAVA. Your mother and I were in the same class at school.

ANNIE. You were in the…you're the same age as my mom?

(YAROSLAVA *winces.*)

YAROSLAVA. To the day. We share a birthday as I recall.

ANNIE. I had no idea, Yaroslava Yanovna.

YAROSLAVA. I imagine there is a lot you can't understand as a happy American child, my sweet niece-*ichka*. We have known very hard times here. Now, sit down.

ANNIE. I don't want to put you out, Yaroslava Yanovna –

YAROSLAVA. Auntie, dear. Your mother promised you to me when you were born – before she ran to a land far, far away. She said I would be your *tyotya*.

ANNIE. I don't want to put you out… Auntie. I can just find a hostel –

YAROSLAVA. After that long journey? *Dyevushka,* you look like you've been to the underworld and back.

ANNIE. The airport was really confusing.

YAROSLAVA. Oh, dear, come here.

(YAROSLAVA *leads* ANNIE *over to the big brick oven.*)

ANNIE. It's embarassing, I started crying like I'm not an adult or something –

YAROSLAVA. You don't need to be an adult, dear. Now, hop up –

ANNIE. What is this?

(*wince*)

YAROSLAVA. My big brick oven. It gets so cold in the apartment, even in summer. It's a good thing you have that heavy fur coat. I usually sleep up here myself.

ANNIE. I don't know…

YAROSLAVA. It's the coziest little *myesta* around.

(*ANNIE slips into place.*)

ANNIE. Ohhhhh, this feels just right.

YAROSLAVA. Are you hungry, dear?

ANNIE. Oh, I'm okay.

YAROSLAVA. I've cooked up a regular feast. Meaty borsch that will stick to your ribs, giant dumplings that will keep you warm for days and a hunk of my homemade bread.

ANNIE. Oh my god, yes.

(*YAROSLAVA begins to exit.*)

YAROSLAVA. (*offstage*) So what exactly brings you all the way here from America? Your mother mentioned school.

ANNIE. Oh, I'm going to be taking, like, Russian lessons.

YAROSLAVA. (*offstage*) But you're speaking Russian right now, dear. What will you learn?

(*YAROSLAVA re-enters and sets a plate down in front of ANNIE. She begins to eat, still reclining, greedily. The food is amazing.*)

ANNIE. I'm supposed to get rid of my American accent and learn more like grown-up words. Like business vocabulary. My Russian is like rust?

YAROSLAVA. You do sound funny. But I knew you were Russian before you opened your mouth. You have the *smell* of the Rus about you.

ANNIE. I wear a body spray.

YAROSLAVA. Oh, no, these were your bones I smelled, dear.

ANNIE. (*mouth full*) My what – ?

(*A wince as YAROSLAVA brushes a piece of hair out of ANNIE's face.*)

YAROSLAVA. No one's fed you in a very long time, have they, dear?

(beat)

ANNIE. No.

Thank you, Yaroslava Yanovna.

YAROSLAVA. Auntie.

ANNIE. Auntie.

Thank you.

6. "Seven-Year-Old Daughter."

(**KATYA**, *19, enters.*)

KATYA. *Zhili byli.*

Once upon a time (they lived, they were)
Two brothers: One rich, one poor.
Because that's just the way it is:
All that emerging middle class stuff is propaganda.
One day, the brothers had an argument –
Something about a horse and a cart,
I won't bore you with old-fashioned details.

Things turned ugly fast and the brothers ended up in court.
Now, the rich man knew how the world works,
so he decided to solve the problem *pa chelovyecheski* –
which means "in the human style" –
which means he slipped a few hundred rubles in his passport before handing it to the judge.
(What can I say? Even fairytales involve bribes.)
The judge, of course, found for the rich man,
but the poor man appealed the decision
and somehow convinced the tsar himself to hear the case.

When the men arrived at the palace,
The Tsar said: I have four riddles for you to solve.
What is stronger and faster than anything on earth?
What is fattiest?
What is softest?
And what is dearer, sweeter, and lovelier than anything else in the world?
Return to me in three days with your answers.

That night, the poor man returned home, crying bitter tears.
As he entered his hut, he met his daughter, his *dochka.*

She was seven years old and her name was Katya.

(gestures to self:)

(Menya zavut Katya.)

And she said: *Batyushka,* little father, why are you crying?

And he answered: The tsar has given me four riddles to solve.

Katya, who was never one for bullshit, said:

Batyushka, dry your tears already and tell me the riddles.

She listened and sat quietly for a second, and then she answered:

The wind is stronger and faster than anything on earth.

The soil is the fattiest –

It doesn't grow, it doesn't live, it just sucks up nourishment.

A hand is the softest –

after all, no matter what else a man lies down on, he always puts his hand under his head.

And the thing that is dearer, sweeter, and lovelier than anything else in the world?

That is a dream.

Three days later, the poor man returned to the tsar

and repeated to him the seven-year-old Katya's answers.

Now, the tsar also had a seven-year-old daughter.

Her name was also Katya.

*(The **OTHER KATYA** enters. **KATYA** sizes her up.)*

OTHER KATYA. *(Menya zavut Katya.)*

KATYA. The tsar said: Your Katya is a little sage.

Go home and repeat this riddle to her.

Ask her: Who is the happiest *dyevochka* in the whole world?

Return to me in the morning with her answer.

The poor man returned home, crying bitter tears.

When Katya saw him, she said:

Batyushka, don't cry.

She wanted to say: Pull yourself the fuck together.

She'd been functioning as the parent in this relationship since she was four –

and it was getting really old.

But she just listened and sat quietly for a second, and then began packing for the morning's journey.

(**KATYA** *delivers the following to the* **OTHER KATYA**.)

When Katya and her father arrived at the palace, they were at once granted an audience with the Other Katya and *her* father,

who raised an eyebrow at our little Katya and said: "Well?"

The happiest *dyevochka* in the whole world, Katya answered,

is your Katya, of course.

For she is the only little girl on earth to have a tsar as her father.

She will be the happiest *dyevochka* in the whole world until she is your 17-year-old daughter,

at which point the happiest *dyevushka* will be me.

You? The tsar asked.

Yes, Katya smiled, for you will be so impressed with me today, you will decide to take me for yourself.

To raise as a daughter with your Katya.

(**KATYA** *takes the* **OTHER KATYA**'s *hand*.)

And we two Katyas will be very happy together.

And when I grow up and am your Other 17-year-old Katya,

You will take me as your bride and make me *tsaritsa*.

This will make me, Katya, the happiest girl in the whole world:

The only *dyevushka* to have a tsar as a father and a husband.

(**KATYA** *and the* **OTHER KATYA** *look at each other*.)

OTHER KATYA. *(to* **KATYA***)* The end.

(The **PROFESSOR***, a middle-aged woman in a frumpy jumper and huge, plastic-framed glasses enters. The past twenty years have passed her by. She refers to the* **KATYA***s as an illustration.)*

PROFESSOR. In Russian *skazki,* there are no fairies and there is no "happily ever after". Endings are frequently happy and formulaic, as in the folktale "The Seven-Year-Old Daughter," but that phrase is not used. Of course, there are also unhappy endings.

(The **KATYA***s exit;* **BABA YAGA** *enters as an illustration.)*

This leads me to an examination of the figure of Baba Yaga with the Bony Leg. Depictions of Baba Yaga vary widely from tale to tale – when a prince encounters her on his hero's journey, she is often a helpful, grandmotherly figure. But woe is the little girl who is sent to Baba Yaga's hut atop tall chicken legs by a stepmother or stepsister – especially if that person claims Baba Yaga as a relative.

*(***ANNIE** *enters, hand raised.)*

ANNIE. Um?

7. "Russian for Business."

(ANNIE's classroom. She sits in the front row.)

PROFESSOR. Yes, Anya? Our only *dyevushka* has a question.

ANNIE. Yes, I just wanted to say. Well, the guys and I –

(gestures to the men behind her)

Joe, Derek, Eric, and Alastair – were talking on the break.

About the fact that this was advertised as a Russian for Business class?

PROFESSOR. That's true, Anya.

ANNIE. And we don't seem to have really learned anything applicable to business?

PROFESSOR. There were good days, the Khrushchev days, when a class like this would not have existed.

Because everyone understood that literature has value –

and it did not need to be marketed as a means to more money.

That was a time when people read real books on the metro:

Turgenev, Pushkin, Dostoevsky, Tolstoy.

And everything was free:

Art, education, museums.

Everything worth something cost nothing.

(beat)

ANNIE. That sounds…kind of beautiful, actually.

PROFESSOR. Well, the *skazka* is over now, thanks to your country. As I was saying, Baba Yagas…

Both evil and kind Baba Yagas use tasks – tedious chores that require magic for completion – to instruct or test their charges.

BABA YAGA. *Dyevushka!*

(PROFESSOR *exits.*)

ANNIE. Yaroslava?

BABA YAGA. *Dyevushka?*

ANNIE. Auntie Yaroslava, I'm right here.

> (**ANNIE** *is in* **YAROSLAVA**'s *apartment.* **BABA YAGA** *is* **YAROSLAVA**.)

YAROSLAVA. Did you reach your mama, dear?

ANNIE. I was gonna finish cleaning these poppy seeds for you first. I've got another kilo to go.

YAROSLAVA. What a good girl! I'm baking bread at daybreak.

ANNIE. Yum. But, um. I was thinking. Picking out each speck of dirt individually doesn't seem like the most efficient way to go about cleaning poppy seeds. What if I rinsed them?

> (**YAROSLAVA** *winces.*)

Or what if I just bought you clean poppy seeds at the store?

> (**YAROSLAVA** *winces.*)

I feel like someone added dirt to this bag you got.

YAROSLAVA. I'm sorry if my dirty food disgusts you…

ANNIE. No, no, I *love* your food. I just thought –

YAROSLAVA. This is the way it's done.

ANNIE. Yeah, yeah, totally.

> (**YAROSLAVA** *picks up a bag of trash leaking a brownish red liquid.*)

YAROSLAVA. I'm going to go dispose of these remains in the garbage chute.

ANNIE. Let me get that for you, Auntie.

YAROSLAVA. No need.

ANNIE. No, Auntie, I insist.

> (**ANNIE** *grabs the bag;* **YAROSLAVA** *hangs on, remembering a second too late not to reveal her true strength.* **ANNIE** *looks a bit surprised.*)

YAROSLAVA. All right, sweet niece. Just remember to stick to the path.

> (**YAROSLAVA** *lets go of the bag and exits.*)

8. "Taking out the Trash."

(In the hall, **MASHA** *is crouched in the corner by the garbag chute, smoking a cigarette. She wears a red hoodie over her nightgown and the red thigh-high boots from earlier.)*

ANNIE. Hey, it's you!

MASHA. Shhhhhh!

ANNIE. Sorry, it's just, we both have *red hoodies* –

*(***ANNIE*** gestures to her sweatshirt.)*

MASHA. *(angry whisper)* What don't you understand about: *Shhhhhhhhhh?!?!*

*(***ANNIE*** moves quickly to the garbage chute to throw out the bag and leave.)*

ANNIE. *(whisper)* Sorry.

MASHA. C'mere.

ANNIE. Sorry?

MASHA. Over here.

*(***ANNIE***, bag still in hand, walks quietly over to* **MASHA**. **MASHA** *gestures for her to come closer and* **ANNIE** *bends over a little to hear.)*

I'm just trying to not wake him. I've been waiting for him to drink himself to sleep for four hours so I could come out for a smoke break.

ANNIE. Who's sleeping? Your father?

MASHA. I almost wish. My dad was a sorry bastard, God rest his soul.

*(***MASHA*** crosses herself, Orthodox style.)*

But at least he was human, y'know?

*(***ANNIE*** stands up to go.)*

ANNIE. Okay, well, good luck.

MASHA. Where are you going? You haven't had a smoke with me yet.

*(***MASHA*** pats the ground next to her and* **ANNIE** *sits down, excitedly.)*

ANNIE. I was sure I saw you that first day I moved in –

(MASHA *gives her a cigarette and lights it for* ANNIE
who takes a very inexpert drag on it. MASHA *looks on
in judgment.*)

ANNIE. Sorry if this sounds weird, my Russian is like rust,
but I've been kind of keeping one eye open for you –

MASHA. Why do you talk funny?

ANNIE. Oh, um, my accent is. We left when I was a kid.
Now I'm American. From Los Angeles.

MASHA. You left? How'd you leave?

ANNIE. Oh, like? Religious asylum, I guess. I'm Jewish.

MASHA. Why?

ANNIE. Why am I Jewish? I don't know, I was born that way.
My name is Anya, by the way. Or Annie.

MASHA. Masha.

ANNIE. So, who are you hiding from, Masha?

MASHA. Well obviously, Misha.

ANNIE. Misha is your boyfriend?

MASHA. Misha is a bear.

ANNIE. Sorry, my Russian's like rust. I thought you said
Misha was a –

MASHA. *Medved.* He didn't used to be. Back in the day,
we used to sit next to each other in class. And then I
found out that he had his own apartment.

ANNIE. This is high school?

MASHA. His parents bit it when he was sixteen and he was
the only one left registered to the place.
I got myself moved in six months later.

ANNIE. Wow.

MASHA. That's not even the wow part.
Zhili byli one night this April, I was studying for
cybernetics...
when I heard a weird noise coming out of the bedroom.
It was a deep, rumbling growl that shook the whole
apartment.

I thought maybe something was attacking Misha, so I grabbed a pot from the kitchen and I opened the bedroom door.

(**MASHA** *pauses. She is starting to enjoy the rhythms of storytelling again – it's been a while.*)

ANNIE. And?

MASHA. And I saw…there, in the bed where Misha had been sleeping, a huge brown bear.

He was wearing Misha's shredded pajama top and was trying to eat the quilt.

ANNIE. No.

MASHA. Yes.

He took me by the throat and said: *Dyevushka!*

If you make a move or sound, I will eat you.

This was two months ago. I've been living with a bear ever since.

ANNIE. But how…how do you live with a bear?

MASHA. Well, I dropped out of university when Misha wouldn't let me go to classes. He had to withdraw, too…because, duh, he's a bear. Now, he sits in the apartment and drinks all day.

ANNIE. Masha, leave! You should leave.

MASHA. He'll eat my mother if I go anywhere.

ANNIE. That's crazy.

MASHA. I know! Cuz I should have held out for more, like my friend Katya. The guy she fucks, he's got so much money, we call him the tsar.

ANNIE. What does he do?

MASHA. Hell if I know. He was Soviet Minister of something, now he's President and CEO of that same thing. He got Katya an apartment in the center. You should see the toilets in this place: 24-karat gold.

ANNIE. Is he handsome?

MASHA. He's fifty. I don't know, I can't tell what's handsome when they get that old. But, really, it doesn't matter, because I could cum just thinking about the handbags he gives her. I am so attracted to this new Louis Vuitton bag she just got. The buttery, pebbled leather, oh my god, it's beautiful. Katya's life is perfect. Except for the tsar's wife, Valentina. Fucking wicked witch.

ANNIE. Oh my god. Her boyfriend is…married.

MASHA. Yeah, of course. He's 50.

ANNIE. Right.

MASHA. My friend Nastya used to say: They all get married at 19, then spend the rest of their lives chasing after 19 year olds. And she should know. She's a whore.

ANNIE. Nastya is – are you really friends with a whore?

MASHA. *Was* friends. Nastya doesn't have a lot of free time anymore. But she's one tough cunt. If I was ever in real trouble, I'd know where to go.

ANNIE. Sure.

MASHA. Listen, can you go out? Does the lady in 57 let you go wherever you want?

ANNIE. *(indignant)* I should hope so. I'm twenty years old and, you know, I'm an American citizen.

MASHA. I ask because I've already got an alibi for Saturday night. Misha promised to let me go to church services this week. And I've got a bottle of the good shit I've been hiding, so he'll be hibernating, guaranteed. Plus, I want you to meet Katya, she'll be so jealous.

ANNIE. Of me?

MASHA. The tsar was planning to take her to L.A. last year when Valentina found out and got Katya's visa pulled.

ANNIE. Wow, I can't believe… Your lives are so, like…

MASHA. Mind-blowing, right?

ANNIE. Totally. I mean, this is pretty much the most fucked-up shit I've ever heard.

(**MASHA** *looks down at her nightgown and stumps out her cigarette.*)

MASHA. Listen, I think I made a mistake. About you.

ANNIE. Sorry, I didn't mean –

MASHA. Y'know, I don't usually dress like this, I was just making a quick exit.

ANNIE. It's not a big – I practically live in sweats.

MASHA. I just don't want you to think,

since you're not from around here –

I just don't want you to think *this* is who I am.

ANNIE. Oh, I don't think anything –

MASHA. Like they say, don't carry your garbage out of your own hut

if you don't want strangers rifling through it.

(**ANNIE** *steps toward the garbage chute, blocking* **MASHA**'s *exit. A challenge:*)

ANNIE. But don't you – ? I mean, you gotta throw your trash out somewhere, right?

(**ANNIE** *steps around* **MASHA** *to throw the garbage bag down the chute. It clanks down several stories.* **ANNIE** *walks back toward the door to* **YAROSLAVA**'s *apartment.*)

Anyway, it was nice to – maybe I'll see you around.

MASHA. Maybe.

(*A beat.*)

I mean, for sure on Saturday night.

ANNIE. What?

MASHA. You *are* going out with me, right? Y'know, to (*knowingly*) church services.

(**ANNIE** *doesn't look at her.*)

ANNIE. *Zhili byli.*

(**ANNIE** *turns to* **MASHA**.)

I guess.

MASHA. Cool.

(**MASHA** *exits.* **ANNIE** *squeals silently.*)

ANNIE. I've never gotten dressed for church before. I don't own a scarf. Or, you know, I own a scarf, but not the kind you put on your head.

9. "Post-lunch Lunch."

(YAROSLAVA's *apartment.* YAROSLAVA *enters, wearing a headscarf, and carrying a frumpy outfit.*)

YAROSLAVA. *Dyevushka, nashla!* I found it.

ANNIE. So, Russian Orthodox women cover their hair as a sign of modesty, right?

(YAROSLAVA *winces;* ANNIE *covers her mouth in response.*)

Sorry, Auntie. Are questions…not cool?

(YAROSLAVA *cringes as she tips* ANNIE's *head down to put the scarf on her head.*)

YAROSLAVA. Here you are, dear.

ANNIE. I just want to be respectful.

YAROSLAVA. Of course, dear.

(YAROSLAVA *starts to help* ANNIE *dress.*)

ANNIE. I mean, church is as new to you guys as the synagogue was to us when we got to L.A. Religion was illegal here and then, one day, everyone wakes up and not only had God come into existence overnight, but He's also like supposed to be the most important thing in your universe. I totally appreciate how weird that is.

(ANNIE *looks down at the clothes.*)

Oh, wow, this is –

YAROSLAVA. Chin down.

ANNIE. *Old.* Like older than my mom probably.

YAROSLAVA. The scarf has known very hard times here. Unlike your mother.

ANNIE. I've got like *history* on my head.

(YAROSLAVA *looks at* ANNIE *in full garb.*)

YAROSLAVA. *(approving)* Indeed. Very nice, dear.
Anya, you should eat something before you go.

ANNIE. *Tyotya,* I'm stuffed – we just had lunch.

YAROSLAVA. You're a growing girl. Just a few bites of sweet *sloika*, a few crumbs of buttery, flaky pastry and a little bit of sticky strawberry filling.

ANNIE. Mmmmmm, I really do like your *sloiki*.

(YAROSLAVA *produces a pastry from her pocket.*)

YAROSLAVA. They're still warm.

ANNIE. Maybe just a bite?

YAROSLAVA. Of course.

(YAROSLAVA *feeds her the pastry.* ANNIE *gobbles it up.*)

ANNIE. *(chewing)* Mmmmmmmm.

(YAROSLAVA *takes a pastry out of her other pocket.*)

YAROSLAVA. Oh, what's this here in my other pocket? Oh, dear, I'd almost forgotten. I made *sloiki* with chocolate filling, too.

ANNIE. *(still chewing)* Chocolate?

YAROSLAVA. Maybe just a bite?

ANNIE. Mmmmhhhhhhhmmmmmm.

(YAROSLAVA *feeds her the other pastry.*)

ANNIE. *(mouth full)* So gooood.

YAROSLAVA. Good, good, eat up. Good girl.

ANNIE. *(mouth still full)* Thank you, Auntie. This is so nice. I never really knew my grandparents, you know.

YAROSLAVA. *(feeding her another bite)* Most of the children I've come across didn't.

ANNIE. *(chewing)* You know, my dad's mom is still alive even. She moved to Tennessee with him. She has cuter grandchildren now. This is just…it's nice.

YAROSLAVA. Good, good, eat up.

(YAROSLAVA *exits.* ANNIE *turns.*)

ANNIE. *Dyevushki,* wait up.

10. "Running in Red Square."

(**ANNIE** *is inserted into a postcard: Red Square, midday, St. Basil's Cathedral in the background.* **KATYA** *and* **MASHA** *enter, wearing headscarves, miniskirts, and little tops. They teeter in stilettos on the cobblestones;* **MASHA** *is wearing her red boots. They hold onto each other as they hobblerun, giddy.*)

MASHA. *(laughing)* Annichka, hurry! He'll catch up!

KATYA. He'll put his grimy paws all over you if you don't run!

ANNIE. *(not moving)* Why are you running away from a guy we stood there and flirted with for twenty minutes?

MASHA. Ooooh, Anya, better move fast before he comes to gobble you up!

(**MASHA** *and* **KATYA** *die of laughter.*)

KATYA. Yeah, he'll eat you up. And then he'll digest you! The acid juices of his stomach will dissolve you and then he'll push you out through his intestinal tubing to his butt and then you'll come out as –

MASHA. *(hyperventilating with laughter)* Don't say it! Don't say it! Don't –

KATYA. She'll come out as –

MASHA. NOOOOO! DON'T SAY IT!

KATYA. *(whispers)* Poop.

MASHA. No! You said it.

(beat)

ANNIE. I don't get it. That doesn't even make any sense.

(**KATYA** *and* **MASHA** *double over with laughter as they try to run.*)

What's the joke?

MASHA. Come HERE, Annichka! Quickly, run!

(**KATYA** *and* **MASHA** *continue their mad, teetering progress.* **ANNIE** *takes a few easy steps in her flats and* *catches up.* **KATYA** *and* **MASHA** *both drape themselves over her for support. The three start to move as one;* **ANNIE** *does all the work.)*

MASHA. My sweet Anya!

KATYA. Little Annichka!

MASHA. You're so fast.

KATYA. And strong.

ANNIE. Not really. I'm just wearing sensible shoes.

(**KATYA** *and* **MASHA** *look at her feet.)*

KATYA. The shoes!

MASHA. Eeew, the shoes!

KATYA. Why are you wearing such ugly shoes?

ANNIE. I don't know, I thought I was getting dressed for church.

MASHA. We can't take her anywhere dressed like this.

KATYA. We'll walk to my apartment and get her better clothes.

MASHA. My feet are killing me. Let's get a car.

KATYA. But, Mashenka, our Anya is an ox. She'll carry us.

MASHA. Omigod, that guy was cute. I should have given him my number.

ANNIE. You're not seriously talking about the guy we just ran away from?

MASHA. You're right. Cute doesn't cut it anymore. Misha used to be cute. I need a tsar like in the end of *skazki*.

KATYA. *Zolushka.*

ANNIE. The Russian Cinderella?

MASHA. Or the best fairytale of all…

KATYA. Yes!

ANNIE. What's better than Cinderella?

KATYA. Poor Annichka, you've never heard of the *Supermodelskaya Skazka.*

ANNIE. The tale of a supermodel?

(**KATYA** *and* **MASHA** *are so excited, their exchange is rapid fire.* **ANNIE** *can't quite keep up.)*

KATYA. Not just any supermodel. *The* supermodel.

MASHA. Natalia Vodianova.

ANNIE. Who?

KATYA. Natalia Vodianova.

ANNIE. I don't really pay attention to who's in the picture. They all look the same.

MASHA. Katyoosha, tell her!

KATYA. She's the fairest of them all.

MASHA. She used to work as a dirty vegetable seller at a dirty market. But she was so lovely that she was discovered at age fifteen and made a model.

ANNIE. That's nice.

MASHA. That's not the best part. She met an English lord.

KATYA. Which is not quite a tsar –

MASHA. But not bad.

ANNIE. And they lived happily ever after.

(In **KATYA**'s *apartment.* **KATYA** *starts throwing possible outfits at* **ANNIE**. *Clothing piles up in her arms.)*

Oh, my god, this is a *makeover!*

MASHA. Try this. I love this.

KATYA. I've been thinking about it, though, and I don't think it's exactly happily ever after.

MASHA. Yeah, I heard divorce rumors.

ANNIE. This is still the Tale of the Supermodel?

KATYA. Marrying a lord is nice, but it would be better to be the daughter of a lord. That way, she is what she is just because she is who she is. You see? Not because she fucked her way into anything, but just because she was born.

MASHA. She had his kids. I think that's not too bad.

KATYA. But isn't it better to *be* his kid? You can take back handbags and apartments –

MASHA. Don't even joke about that!

KATYA. I wouldn't. But the thing is: You can never take back blood.

(**ANNIE** *holds clothes up to herself, gauging size. She starts trying a few things on.*)

ANNIE. This guy from class, Eric or Derek, I don't remember which, said that there's an old Russian saying about a man who asks a woman to sleep with him for a million dollars. She thinks about it for a second and then agrees. Then he asks her to sleep with him for a hundred dollars and she slaps him. So he says: What? We've already established that you're a whore, now we're just negotiating the price.

KATYA. Who said that?

ANNIE. *(nervous)* Um, one of the guys from my Russian for Business class.

They're just these loser guys who have come to

Rus to reap their rewards and pick out a mail-order bride in person.

KATYA. These are Americans?

ANNIE. But they're total losers.

KATYA. See, that just doesn't make sense. That's not how you wear it.

(**KATYA** *adjusts the garment* **ANNIE** *is trying on.*)

ANNIE. Like I said, they're just asshole –

KATYA. No, I mean economically. *Dyevushki* are not dying to run off to – I don't know, South Dakota – for a few thousand dollars.

(**KATYA** *starts undoing the piece of clothing* **ANNIE** *is trying on.*)

That isn't right. Try on something else. I mean, what's the median household income in the U.S.?

ANNIE. I have no idea.

KATYA. If I remember correctly, it's about 45,000 dollars. In Moscow alone, there are at least twenty-five billionaires. Why would a *dyevushka* run after an American? Better to aim for a Russian billionaire.

ANNIE. Wow, you know a lot about income stuff.

MASHA. Katya was studying on the Economics *facultyet* at the University.

KATYA. Until the tsar decided that interior design was a more appropriate course of study for a girlfriend. This doesn't look right, either.

ANNIE. It's too small. I've gotten so fat lately.

MASHA. You're not fat.

KATYA. Medically speaking.

ANNIE. All the *dyevushki* here are so skinny. And my *tyotya* Yaroslava just keeps feeding me. She's been waking me up in the middle of the night with pieces of the most delicious gingerbread.

MASHA. You know, I've never seen her go out the door.

ANNIE. Seriously? There's always food.

KATYA. Maybe she doesn't go out the door.

ANNIE. What, she's flying out the window at night?

KATYA. That's what witches do.

ANNIE. *(joking around)* She does have a large broom.

MASHA. Russian witches don't fly on brooms. They sit on giant mortars and use giant pestles to paddle through the air.

ANNIE. So, there you go.

KATYA. No, they don't fly *on* brooms. But they do carry them to sweep away their tracks from the sky.

(KATYA *pulls out a dress.*)

Here, try this. This is oversized, but still sexy.

(ANNIE *slips the dress over her head.*)

ANNIE. *(dress covering her face)* So, what am I supposed to do? Sleep with one eye open to see if the old woman I'm living with is actually flying out the window on a giant mortar and pestle?

KATYA. I'd just be curious as to how she affords so much food. *Pensioniri* live on a hundred bucks a month in Moscow. How does that fit?

ANNIE. Better, I think.

(MASHA *stands in front of* ANNIE *to finish the makeover, blocking her from view. A cell phone rings: The theme from Sex and the City.*)

KATYA. Oh, that's me.

(She answers the phone.)

Allyo.

(Silence. **VALENTINA***, 42, enters, breathing heavily. She is dressed all in expensive-looking black.* **KATYA** *looks at the other girls and steps away to take the call.* **KATYA** *talks into the phone, but addresses* **VALENTINA** *directly.)*

Valentina, I know it's you. No one else calls me just to pant into the phone.

VALENTINA. *(so angry she creaks and hisses)* Stay. Away.

KATYA. I think your 800-calorie apple diet is making you crazy. He's not here right now, try calling someone else.

VALENTINA. Not. *Him.* I. Don't. Give a Shit. About *Him.* Stay. The Hell. Away. From *Her.*

*(***KATYA*** *freezes up: she's been caught.)*

KATYA. I don't know what you're talking about.

VALENTINA. I know your smell, you filthy slut. The smell of your bones and that disgusting body spray. I've been smelling it on him for the last two years. And then: Last night, I smelled it on my daughter.

KATYA. I didn't do anything, I swear. I was out at a café and I saw her.

(The **OTHER KATYA** *enters.* **KATYA** *looks at her, mesmerized.)*

I recognized her immediately from the picture in his wallet.

Oh my god, she is so beautiful my eyes started burning like I was staring at the sun. It sounds crazy or clichéd but I'd really never seen anything like her.

The Other Katya.

(The **OTHER KATYA** *approaches her.)*

I couldn't help it, I went over to talk to her.

I didn't say who I was, just asked her questions.

How does she like being called Katya?

Does she love her father? Is he kind to her?

What is it like, going to the Economics Institute?

I told her that I had dreamed of going there once,

that a man had promised me he would help me with it,

but then decided, I don't know, I wasn't worthy.

I asked her: What do you dream about?

Because I think a dream is the dearest, sweetest, loveliest thing in the world,

and I'd like to know what is dearest, sweetest, loveliest to you.

And she told me she dreams of numbers:

Sequences of numbers that she scans for patterns in her sleep.

And I wanted to cry, because that's the way I dream, too.

VALENTINA. I do not want you to see her again, you understand?

(**KATYA** *reaches out to touch the* **OTHER KATYA**'s *hair.*)

KATYA. That's like asking me to never look in a mirror ever again. I might accidentally –

VALENTINA. You listen to me, you little whore: I have tolerated you. Knowing that everything he gives you – that apartment, those handbags – everything he gives to you, he is taking away from my Katya.

KATYA. Does Katya want any purses? I'd love to give her –

VALENTINA. You stay the fuck away from her. Or else you'll see what kind of wicked witch I can be.

(**VALENTINA** *hangs up the phone and walks away.* **KATYA** *looks at the* **OTHER KATYA**.)

KATYA. I thought I might find you here.

(**OTHER KATYA** *kisses her once on each cheek in greeting.*)

OTHER KATYA. You made it!

KATYA. I brought friends. Masha!

11. "Girls' Night Out."

(*A nightclub with Russian rap music thumping in the background; it's just loud enough that it can't be spoken over comfortably.* **KATYA** *gestures to* **MASHA** *to come closer, revealing* **ANNIE***'s makeover. She's completely transformed, wearing a short dress, stilettos, and carrying a designer purse.*)

OTHER KATYA. HI.

KATYA. Katya, meet my friend Masha. I've known this *dyevushka* since…when?

MASHA. What are you doing?

KATYA. How long exactly have we known each other?

MASHA. Since always.

KATYA. This is Anya. She lives in California.

OTHER KATYA. I spent last summer in Connecticut, my dad sent me to language camp there to get rid of my accent.

ANNIE. That's funny, that's why I'm here.

KATYA. That's so great that your dad sees your potential.

MASHA. Katya, can we talk in private?

OTHER KATYA. (*to* **ANNIE**) I like your bag!

ANNIE. It's Katya's.

OTHER KATYA. I have the same one, my dad brought it back from Paris.

MASHA. *Katya!*

ANNIE. This club is AWESOME. I don't think I've ever seen so many beautiful people in one room before.

OTHER KATYA. It's a little dead tonight.

ANNIE. We should drink! I love being able to drink legally. The U.S. is so stupid about that.

KATYA. (*to* **MASHA**) Why don't you go get Annie cocktails?

OTHER KATYA. (*to* **ANNIE**) I know, right? I mean, it's just alcohol.

MASHA. Why don't you give me money to do that?

(**KATYA** *hands* **MASHA** *a credit card.*)

ANNIE. The thing I don't get is: What's up with all the girls at the bar with their teacups? Why wouldn't you drink if you can?

MASHA. *(looking at* **KATYA***)* They're whores. They don't want to spend money on drinks before they make money on dicks.

KATYA. Masha! Katya's not accustomed to that kind of language.

(**MASHA** *pulls* **ANNIE.***)*

MASHA. C'mon, Annie.

(They exit.)

KATYA. Let's go somewhere quieter so we can actually talk.

(They step outside. The **OTHER KATYA** *takes out a "Vogue" cigarette and* **KATYA** *helps her light it.)*

This is better.

OTHER KATYA. Yeah. I can't stay out late anyway. I have to study tomorrow.

KATYA. What's your test on?

OTHER KATYA. You don't really want to know. You'll think it's boring.

KATYA. I want to know so badly my teeth hurt from wanting to know.

OTHER KATYA. *(laughs)* I love how crazy you are.

KATYA. The pain is moving into my gums…

OTHER KATYA. It's on money supply.

KATYA. That sounds wonderful.

OTHER KATYA. It is pretty cool. It's just really stressful – my mom freaks out about my grades. It's weird because economics is my dad's thing really, but, you know, she can't make him happy herself so she tries to make him happy through me. My mom is fucked up, I hate her.

KATYA. You *hate* her?

OTHER KATYA. I HATE her!

KATYA. I hate her, too.

OTHER KATYA. I just hate living with her, you know?

KATYA. I live by myself.

OTHER KATYA. Seriously? You're so lucky. I want to come live with you.

KATYA. That'd be great.

OTHER KATYA. In a million years. We could totally afford an apartment in the center, but my mom will never let me move out of her monster mansion in Rublovka.

KATYA. What if you didn't ask her?

OTHER KATYA. It wouldn't matter. She's a crazy bitch, she'd come kidnap me back. Ugh, god, I could kill her, you know? Sometimes.

KATYA. *I* could kill her.

OTHER KATYA. You couldn't.

KATYA. I could.

OTHER KATYA. She's got a shit ton of security.

KATYA. I've never met a riddle I couldn't solve.

(**OTHER KATYA** *laughs.*)

OTHER KATYA. Omigod, you're insane, I love it. Let's get a drink.

(**OTHER KATYA** *starts to exit, but* **KATYA** *grabs her hand.*)

KATYA. Katya?

OTHER KATYA. Yes, Katya?

KATYA. Let me get this, I'll take care of everything for you. Like magic.

OTHER KATYA. Oooooh, I like magic.

(**OTHER KATYA** *exits; the thumping music is momentarily louder as the offstage door to the club swings open, then returns to a more muted level.*)

KATYA. Think of it like a riddle.

(**ANNIE** *enters, balancing shots, precariously.* **MASHA** *follows behind her, sizing up the* **OTHER KATYA** *as she exits.*)

Every clever heroine knows –

ANNIE. I have, um, shots!

MASHA. You wanna disappear like you were never here?

ANNIE. If you, like, tip your head back –

KATYA. *(to* **MASHA***)* Hello to you, too.

MASHA. You think you're special. You're not special.

ANNIE. You can get 'em down in just one –

KATYA. I know what I'm doing.

MASHA. It's not like you're even gonna be the only body buried in that bitch's backyard.

KATYA. I'm leaving.

ANNIE. *(to* **MASHA***)* Who are you talking about – ?

KATYA. Good night, Annie.

MASHA. And that dumb ass daughter of hers?

KATYA. Don't you talk about –

ANNIE. Are you talking about –

MASHA. – the Other Katya?

ANNIE. *What* is going –

MASHA. She'd order the hit herself if she knew who you really were.

ANNIE. The Other Katya?

MASHA. Is the fucking Tsar's daughter.

ANNIE. Whoa, that's –

KATYA. Just because I didn't settle for the first animal with an apartment –

MASHA. Screw you. I'm trying to help.

KATYA. I don't need your help. I've outgrown you.

ANNIE. Katya, I'm sure you don't mean –

KATYA. Oh, I do.

MASHA. C'mon, Annie, let's go.

(**MASHA** *grabs two shot glasses from* **ANNIE**. *She clinks it together with* **ANNIE**'s.)

MASHA. To friendship.

(**MASHA** *downs the shot and she and* **ANNIE** *exit;* **KATYA** *watches them go.*)

KATYA. Every clever heroine knows.
Action must be taken.
Soon.

12. "Goodnight, Little Ones."

(MASHA *and* ANNIE *enter the hallway on their floor, tipsily.*)

MASHA. I'm deleting her number, don't think I won't!

ANNIE. Shhhhhh.

MASHA. Shhhhhh yourself.

ANNIE. No, seriously, shhhhhh.

MASHA. Oh, right. We don't want to wake up my bear and your witch.

ANNIE. We don't know that she's a –

MASHA. Shhhhhh.

> *(beat)*

Shit.

ANNIE. What's wrong?

MASHA. I call Katya's number three times a day. It's frickin' memorized.

(MASHA *and* ANNIE *glance back at their respective doors.*)

ANNIE. Well, I guess this is us.

MASHA. Unfortunately.

ANNIE. God. You don't really think – she's such a sweet old lady – ?

MASHA. *(shrugs)* Misha was sweet, too.

ANNIE. But this can't be like real danger.
My mom sent me.

MASHA. That's nothing. I complained once and you know what my mom told me? She said: Grow the fuck up. Your father was a bear, too. At least you got an apartment. I had to live with my in-laws for the first ten years.

ANNIE. That's –

MASHA. A hard-knock life.

ANNIE. God, I haven't talked to my mom once since I got here.

(**MASHA** *softens.*)

MASHA. Listen, Annichka, I'm always across the hall. I won't let you disappear like you were never here, okay?

(**ANNIE** *and* **MASHA** *turn toward their respective apartments.* **ANNIE** *takes a big breath and reaches out for the door handle as* **MASHA** *exits.* **ANNIE** *turns back.*)

ANNIE. Mash – ?

(**ANNIE** *sees that she is gone.*)

Sleep with one eye open.

(**ANNIE** *opens the door and enters* **YAROSLAVA**'s *apartment.*)

13. "Alone in the Apartment."

(**ANNIE** *slips off* **KATYA**'s *stilettos and puts down her purse. She notices a breeze and tiptoes over to the open window; she carefully closes the window.*)

(*She cranes her head to see into the corner.*)

ANNIE. *(whispering)* Auntie, are you –

(*She covers her mouth, realizing she was about to ask a question.*)

Oh, crap! Questions really piss her off. How to ask if she's home without a question…oh, god, that's a question.

(*She cranes her head farther.*)

Auntie?

(*A beat. She looks back at the window.*)

How does an old lady with brittle little legs…
Go out through the window in the middle of the night?

(*The window slams shut;* **ANNIE** *jumps.*)

(*She picks up the phone and pulls out a phone card and dials.*)

(**OLGA** *enters.*)

OLGA. Hhhhhello, hahney –

ANNIE. *(overlapping)* Mom?

OLGA. You haf reached Olga Rabinovich. I can't answer phone right now, so please leave message. Annichka, if it's you, *ya tebya ochen lyublyu.* I love you, baby, very much. Keep evil eye close to heart, it ward off dangers.

(*beep*)

ANNIE. Mom? I'm sorry I haven't called earlier… Everything's fine here.

(*She looks at the window.*)

Mostly. But I need to ask you about Yaroslava Yanovna. You said something about wicked –
Mom, what did you – ?

(Beep. **ANNIE** *looks at phone for a beat, then hangs up.)*

(She dials again.)

OLGA. Hhhello, hahney –

ANNIE. *(overlapping)* Mom, are –

OLGA. You haf reached Olga Rabinovich. I can't answer phone right now, so please leave –

*(***ANNIE*** hangs up phone and* **OLGA** *exits.)*

ANNIE. I don't believe in evil eyes.

*(***ANNIE*** runs to dig the fur coat out of her suitcase.)*

I don't believe in evil –

It's gone.

Why is there a hole in its place...

*(***ANNIE*** pulls out the fur and holds it up to look for the pin. Instead, in the place where the pin had been, there is a hole shaped like the USSR.)*

...shaped like the Soviet Union?

(In this instant, **YAROSLAVA** *appears suddenly behind* **ANNIE** *in shadows.)*

YAROSLAVA. *Dyevushka.*

(There is a breeze blowing in from the window again.)

ANNIE. Shit. Where have you been?

(cringe)

YAROSLAVA. Right here, dear.

ANNIE. I saw that window close. You were not in the apartment when that window closed.

YAROSLAVA. Have you been drinking, darling?

ANNIE. I'm an adult, I know what I saw.

YAROSLAVA. You have been drinking, darling.

ANNIE. Where does the food come from?

(cringe)

YAROSLAVA. That's no concern of yours.

ANNIE. Why doesn't anyone ever see you outside?

(cringe)

YAROSLAVA. Look at me. I'm your *tyotya*, dear, but I look withered enough to be your *baba*. You don't think your *baba tyotya* notices when apple-cheeked children stare at her on the street and ask their mothers if she is a wicked witch.

(**ANNIE** *looks down.*)

ANNIE. *Tyotya*, that's so – you shouldn't worry about what other people think like that.

YAROSLAVA. It's a city filled with *dyevushki*. How can I not? I started having groceries delivered some time ago so I wouldn't have to go outside.

ANNIE. I'm sorry, Auntie.

YAROSLAVA. Don't be silly, dear. You'd had too much to drink and you're very tired.

(**YAROSLAVA** *puts an arm around her; her other hand stays at her side, holding on to something.*)

And hungry? Are you hungry, dear?

ANNIE. No thank you.

(*beat*)

When does the grocery delivery come?

(*cringe*)

YAROSLAVA. When you are not here.

(**ANNIE** *looks up at her.*)

What do you think? That I have three magic hands that float through the night and slip into the *gastronom* after closing to steal me the plumpest melons, the bloodiest steaks, the juiciest tomatoes? That sometimes I fly out the window myself?

ANNIE. Why is there a hole in my fur coat?

(*cringe*)

And what happened to my evil eye pin?

(*cringe*)

Did *you* take my evil eye pin? Oh my god, you did, didn't you?

YAROSLAVA. You're very sleepy, dear.

(*ANNIE tries to step away from* **YAROSLAVA***, but she tightens her grip. Offstage, there is a growl coming from* **MASHA***'s apartment.*)

ANNIE. I have to go across the hall to talk to Masha.

YAROSLAVA. It's too late for that kind of silliness.

(*ANNIE looks down at* **YAROSLAVA***'s hand.*)

ANNIE. What is in your hand?

(*Cringe!*)

Why are you holding – oh my god, why are you holding – ?

A pestle!

(**YAROSLAVA** *raises the pestle above her head, about to strike;* **ANNIE***'s bulging eyes look out at the audience. Blackout.*)

14. "A Forbidden Folktale."

(Spotlight up on **NASTYA**.*)*

NASTYA. Now for a little change of pace!
The *Russkiye Zavyetniye Skazki.*
Or, Forbidden Russian Folktales.
These are like state secrets of storytelling.
They were collected by the same guy
who did all the other *skazki.*
Aleksandr Afanasyev. He lived in the 1800s
when you couldn't publish this stuff.
Which is why they're called forbidden.
Which is why they sound so sweet.
Like me.

Zhili byli.
Once up on a time,
they lived, they were
a virgin *dyevushka*
name Anastasia.
Nastya, for short.

(gestures to self:)
(Menya zavut Nastya.)
One day, Nastya was talking to her girlfriend,
her very best *padruga,*
about the future and growing up and
getting the hell out of nowhereville, Russia,
when her friend started talking about getting married.
And our Nastya said: I don't ever want to get married.
I mean, do you know what they do to us?
They stick their big tools into our you-know-whatskis.
No, I'll never get married unless my dad makes me.
And if my dad makes me, I'll only marry a eunuch.

Now it just so happened that at this very moment,

a *malchik* from the village was eavesdropping on the girls' conversation, thinking:

For nowhereville, Russia, this Nastya is kind of a catch.

Her dad was the Mid-level Manager of Procurement at the factory.

So, this *malchick*, let's call him, oh,

I don't know, say, Ivan Idiotivich,

Made sure to beat up a horse really bad

one day in front of our Nastya, so that she would ask:

Why are you beating that poor horse?

And Ivan answered: What can I do with a nag like this?

I'd fuck the shit out of her, but I don't have a prick.

(**NASTYA** *perks up: Hallelujah!*)

In that moment, Nastya new she'd found Mr. Right.

Soon after this, Nastya's father, the Mid-level Manager of Procurement,

was killed by a neighbor in a drunken hunting accident slash weeklong killing spree (depending on which account you believe),

leaving Nastya a defenseless orphan with a little bit of money.

Two days after that, Nastya married Ivan Idiotivich –

and two hours after that he gave it to her until she bled.

She was confused. Uh, tell me, dear, where did this prick come from?

Ivan said: I borrowed it from my uncle for our wedding night.

Nastya thought for a second: Maybe she could get used to this.

Talk to your uncle, dear, and offer to buy his prick so we can keep if for good.

Ivan said: I'm pretty sure my uncle would agree to sell us the cock...for 10,000 rubles.

But where on earth are we going to get that kind of money?

I have a little bit of money from my father, Nastya said.

Ivan's face lit up. Oh, really? I had no idea, he said.

So, Nastya went and took 10,000 rubles from her mattress and gave it to Ivan.

This is for you, my darling husband, she said.

And that was how Nastya went and bought herself a huge prick.

The end.

Or not the end, really, since right after that,
she moved with the huge prick to the big city.
And right after *that*, he left her in the big city alone.
With no money or place to stay or work papers.
So, right after that, she started working as a whore.

(**NASTYA** *takes out a pair of scissors and starts trimming her wig.*)

One day, a man who Nastya knew to be an associate of Ivan Idiotivich came to see her.

In exchange for a deep discount on her services,
this man agreed to tell her the big prick's location.

That night, Nastya went to see Ivan Idiotivich
to demand her cut –
a return of the 10,000 ruble investment.

(**NASTYA** *makes a big cut into the air.*)

Nastya got her purchase back, all right.
And she lived happily ever after.
The end.

(**NASTYA** *exits.*)

15. "Outsmarting a Potato."

(ANNIE *asleep atop the big brick oven. She's still wearing* KATYA*'s mini-dress, but she's got some serious bedhead.*)

YAROSLAVA. *(offstage) Dyevushka*, wake up.

(*One of* ANNIE*'s eyes pops open.*)

Dyevushka.

ANNIE. Uggghhh.

(ANNIE *sits up woozily, as* YAROSLAVA *enters with a tray of food.*)

Byli zhili am I where lived were.

YAROSLAVA. Somebody had a rough night.

Three nights ago.

You've been sleeping for two full days.

ANNIE. Not remember.

YAROSLAVA. I know, dear.

ANNIE. My head.

YAROSLAVA. Food will absorb the alcohol.

ANNIE. More.

YAROSLAVA. Food, dear? Certainly.

ANNIE. No. More than alcohol.

YAROSLAVA. Eat up.

You've been wasting away in your sleep.

(ANNIE *takes a bite as* YAROSLAVA *exits.* ANNIE *jumps down from the brick oven, stumbling as she hits the floor. She tries to stand.*)

YAROSLAVA. *(offstage)* Are you eating, niece?

ANNIE. Yes, am.

(ANNIE *scrambles to the door, opens it quickly and runs out into the hall. She begins pounding on* MASHA*'s door. As quietly as she can:*)

Mash!

(On the other side of the door, the **FIGURE** *in the fur coat lurks.)*

Masha, are you? I'm not well –

*(***ANNIE*** braces herself against the door, pulls herself together.)*

Open the door, Masha.

*(***ANNIE*** knocks again, looking over her shoulder back at* **YAROSLAVA***'s door.)*

Mash, you said sometimes doesn't let you your boyfriend –

(The **FIGURE** *perks up.)*

And you said he's a bear. And now I'm worried that wasn't like…a metaphor. So, open the door, Masha. *Please.*

(The **FIGURE** *reaches for the door handle and is about to turn it when* **YAROSLAVA** *suddenly grabs her from behind.)*

YAROSLAVA. *Dyevushka.*

(The **FIGURE***'s arm drops.)*

Come back inside, it's not safe to wander off the path.

*(***YAROSLAVA*** looks icily at* **MASHA***'s door.)*

ANNIE. Masha!

YAROSLAVA. She's not there, dear.

*(***YAROSLAVA*** starts to lead* **ANNIE** *away from the door.)*

ANNIE. Masha!

YAROSLAVA. You slept through her leaving yesterday. I watched her from the window, packing garbage bags into a *Lada* waiting outside.

ANNIE. No, I heard something breathing –

YAROSLAVA. She took bags and bags out the door, then disappeared like she was never here.

(Lights down on the **FIGURE** *as* **YAROSLAVA** *leads* **ANNIE** *back into her apartment.)*

ANNIE. No! I'm going –
  I'm going school.

YAROSLAVA. You've overslept your class. And you have work
  to do.

ANNIE. I'm calling my mom!

YAROSLAVA. You're welcome to try on my phone.

ANNIE. I'm going out.

YAROSLAVA. After you finish your work. I'll be making a big
  stew soon with lots of potatoes.

  (**YAROSLAVA** *produces a basket of potatoes.*)

  I need you to peel those potatoes.

ANNIE. And then I can leave?

  (cringe)

YAROSLAVA. That's right.

ANNIE. I need the peeler.

YAROSLAVA. Oh, no, the peeler wastes too much valuable
  potato. Use your pretty little fingernails.

  (**ANNIE** *puts a hand to her head and slumps.*)

  You need a snack to keep up your strength.

ANNIE. Not hungry.

YAROSLAVA. Of course you are, dear.

  (**YAROSLAVA** *puts a pastry in front of* **ANNIE***'s face.*
  ANNIE *resists her, so* **YAROSLAVA** *shoves it into her
  mouth.* **ANNIE** *won't chew, so* **YAROSLAVA** *starts moving
  her jaw with her hands. Finally,* **ANNIE** *succumbs to the
  deliciousness of the pastry.*)

ANNIE. *(mouth full)* Mmmmmmm. God, that's good.

YAROSLAVA. Now, get to work. The potatoes will see to it
  that you behave.

  (**YAROSLAVA** *exits.* **ANNIE** *runs back to the door – the
  basket of potatoes follows, cutting her off.*)

ANNIE. Oh, crap.

YAROSLAVA. *(offstage)* Start peeling, *dyevushka!*

(**ANNIE** *tries to take a step around the basket, but it again cuts her off.*)

ANNIE. Oh, crap.

(**ANNIE** *runs toward the phone. The basket follows her again. She picks up a potato and starts scratching at it. To* **YAROSLAVA**:)

Just getting started!

YAROSLAVA. Those potatoes have eyes. Be on your best behavior.

ANNIE. The potatoes have eyes. Oh, crap.

(**ANNIE** *scratches at a potato and edges toward the telephone. She looks back to where* **YAROSLAVA** *exited. She pulls the phone card out of her pocket with one hand and starts dialing.*)

(**OLGA** *enters.*)

OLGA. Hhhhhello, hahney –

ANNIE. This fucking voicemail message!

OLGA. Annie…is that you?

ANNIE. Mom? Mom!

(*The potato in* **ANNIE***'s hand pulls her hand toward the phone and hangs it up. To the potato:*)

Not cool!

(**ANNIE** *begins dialing again, but the potato starts banging at the phone. She throws the potato across the room.*)

OLGA. Hhhello, hahney –

ANNIE. Mom!

(*The potato begins inching across the room to her.*)

OLGA. Annie, baby, are you okay?

ANNIE. Mom: Yaroslava Yanovna. Did she – ? Ma, did she give you that scar?

OLGA. Wicked witches is crazy bitches.

ANNIE. Oh my god, she gave you that scar.

OLGA. I had to leave her you legacy, baby.

ANNIE. My – ? What are you talking about?

OLGA. I'm sorry, I give up you chances for gold toilets –

(*ANNIE looks around.*)

ANNIE. The apartment.

OLGA. I haf to choose.

ANNIE. Like you very own home. Was this *our* apart – ?

OLGA. You legacy.

Or *you*, Annie.

ANNIE. Oh my god.

OLGA. I take you and run far, far away.

I don't ask no questions –

(*The potato flies suddenly at her, causing* **ANNIE** *to drop the phone;* **OLGA** *exits.* **ANNIE** *grabs the potato, which pulls her hand toward the basket and knocks a few other potatoes out, which fly toward* **ANNIE**. *She kicks them away and starts scratching at the first potato in her hand. In turn, the potato pulls her hand to start hitting her in the head.*)

If a *dyevushka* can outwit a witch –

(*She grasps the potato in both hands, struggling to keep it still.*)

How do I outsmart a potato? The potatoes have eyes... I could blindfold them.

(*ANNIE runs to retrieve her fur coat. The basket follows her. She throws the coat over the basket as if trapping an animal. To the potatoes:*)

Okay, now stay.

(*ANNIE takes a few steps. The basket doesn't move. She grabs her sensible shoes and pulls them on. As she's tying her laces, a single potato emerges from the hole in the fur.*)

Oh, crap.

(*ANNIE makes a run for it.*)

16. *"Padrugi"*

(ANNIE *pounds on* KATYA's *door.* KATYA *pokes her head out into the hall.*)

ANNIE. Katya, thank god.

KATYA. What are you doing here?

ANNIE. I need your help!

KATYA. The Tsar is –
This isn't a good time.

ANNIE. But it's about Masha. And, also, my head's really fuzzy – but I think my not-really-aunt knocked me out and then told a basket of fighting potatoes to beat me up.

KATYA. Give me a second.

(KATYA *disappears inside the apartment.*)

ANNIE. There is no such thing as witches, but. There are wicked crazy bitches –

(KATYA *reappears, closing the door quietly behind her.*)

KATYA. Listen, I know I shouldn't have said what I did.
But Masha has to start answering my calls some time.

ANNIE. That's just it. She's not answering the door either.

KATYA. Oh, god.

ANNIE. What? What do you know?

KATYA. I tried calling her mother –

ANNIE. No answer?

KATYA. Until this morning.
Masha's mother's neighbor picked up.
The phone was laying the hallway, she said.
She said: It was covered in what looked like dried blood.

ANNIE. Saturday night, after Masha walked into her apartment, I heard.
I heard growling, Katya.

KATYA. Something is not right here.

ANNIE. What if – when she came home.

KATYA. Mahsa would have walked in and seen a stack of dirty dishes.

(MASHA *enters.*)

MASHA. Somebody's been eating my porridge. Asshole. And somebody's been sitting in my chair. And has shredded the crap out of the upholstery with his dirty claws.

ANNIE. She might've walked into the bedroom.

MASHA. Somebody's been sleeping in my –

KATYA. She would have taken a closer look.

MASHA. No one is sleeping in my bed.

ANNIE. She would trace her steps back through the apartment.

MASHA. Misha?

KATYA. Then the bathroom.

MASHA. Oh, my god, Misha!

(*A faint light on a* FIGURE *in the fur coat, lying facedown on the floor.*)

Misha, what happened?

(MASHA *crouches down next to him to examine him. She touches his fur and blood comes off on her hands.*)

What did you do to yourself?

(MASHA *shakes him.*)

KATYA. But all the bear said was: Girl?

MASHA. Misha, it's me.

ANNIE. She didn't call, he thought she wasn't coming back.

MASHA. I'm sorry.

KATYA. Maybe he thought she'd run off with someone new. She hasn't touched him in such a long time, maybe he's started to think she's disgusted by the way he looks.

MASHA. You shouldn't have hurt yourself, baby.

ANNIE. She told me she was giving him a bottle of vodka.
The good shit they hadn't had in months.

KATYA. He would have been out of his mind.

MASHA. It's not really that I stopped loving you –
It's just that it looked like you'd stopped *being* you.

ANNIE. The bear would close his eyes, which would be very
shiny and wet, and say:
I'm sorry.

(**MASHA** *inspects his fur, looking for the wound to
bandage.*)

MASHA. Where are you bleeding from, baby?
You know the ambulance won't come out here.
You need to tell me where you're bleeding from.

(*She frantically pushes her fingers through his fur.*)

ANNIE. I'm sorry, the bear said.

(**MASHA** *holds up a necklace to the light.*)

MASHA. What is – why do you have my mother's necklace?

KATYA. And then Masha knew

(**MASHA** *wearily gestures to herself:*)

MASHA. (Menya zavut Masha.)

ANNIE. That the blood –

KATYA. – was not coming from the bear.

(*The* **FIGURE** *rises up and envelops* **MASHA** *inside the
coat.* **ANNIE** *and* **KATYA** *look at the* **FIGURE**. **ANNIE**
turns back to **KATYA** *and the* **FIGURE** *disappears.*)

ANNIE. Is that what happened? Does that shit happen?

KATYA. I don't know.

ANNIE. What do we do?

KATYA. I don't know.

ANNIE. How can you not know?

KATYA. Annie, I'm losing the Other Katya.

Valentina told her about me.

Who I really am.

He's inside breaking up with me now.

ANNIE. Oh, Katya, does that mean – ?

KATYA. I'll be out of the apartment by daybreak.

She's making him take back all the handbags, too.

ANNIE. I'm so sorry, Katya. But what do we do? I can't go back to Yaroslava's, but we can't just leave Masha either. We can't let Masha disappear like she was never here.

KATYA. Think of it like a riddle.

ANNIE. What if we go see Nastya?

KATYA. How do you know Nastya?

ANNIE. Masha just said that if she was ever in real trouble, she'd go to Nastya.

KATYA. She *is* one tough cunt.

ANNIE. So, how do we get to her?

KATYA. *(a realization)* Nastya. That's perfect.

(**KATYA** *fishes out a piece of paper and a pen and starts scribbling.*)

Look, Anya, I'm going to tell you something that means we're going to be friends now. I mean, real friends.

ANNIE. Of course.

KATYA. The thing is, I'm not going to go with you now because I'm going to need an alibi later. And I don't know any alibi richer than the tsar.

ANNIE. What?

KATYA. I'll get him to stay a couple hours for old times' sake, then I'll slip something into his before-bed cocktail.

ANNIE. No, you have to come with me.

KATYA. I'll meet you at Masha's later.

ANNIE. I don't think I can do this without you.

KATYA. Annie, you're a grown-up *dyevushka.* Action must be taken.

(**KATYA** *hands her a piece of paper with instructions.*)

This is how you'll find Nastya.

(**KATYA** *folds up a piece of paper into a small square.*)

And this is for her eyes alone.

(**KATYA** *exits.* **ANNIE** *sets out, consulting the piece of paper in her hand several times. She walks up to* **NASTYA**'s *door.*)

17. "The Fairy Godmother."

(ANNIE *knocks.*)

ANNIE. Excuse me? Uh, *menya zavut* Anya and I need help. It's about Masha?

(The door swings open. ANNIE *walks inside.)*

I think Masha is in trouble.

*(*NASTYA, *still in her bathrobe and wig, steps out from behind the door and pins* ANNIE *against the wall.)*

NASTYA. Who the fuck are you and what the fuck are you doing in my apartment?

ANNIE. I got your address from Katya. It's for Masha.

NASTYA. Katya and Masha, huh?

ANNIE. Yeah, I'm a friend.

NASTYA. Those backstabbing bitches.

ANNIE. They said you're a friend –

NASTYA. *Was.* I haven't heard from those sluts in months.

ANNIE. They said that if they were ever really in troubles they would come to you.

NASTYA. So, then? Where are they? Why did they send some chick who talks funny? What's wrong with you anyway?

ANNIE. I'm American.

NASTYA. Perfect. They send a fucking American!

ANNIE. Nastya, I'm sorry that they haven't been in touch, but I think that Masha can't be in touch right now. It's Misha.

*(*NASTYA *lets go of* ANNIE *and is suddenly serious.)*

NASTYA. Take a seat.

ANNIE. What do you know about Misha?

NASTYA. He was a friend of my bastard ex-husband Ivan. Fucking idiot. That's how I met those *dyevushki.*

ANNIE. I guess within the last few months, Misha has changed a lot. He's... Masha said he'd become a bear.

(NASTYA *nods, but doesn't say anything.*)

That sounds insane, but... I haven't seen her and Katya talked to Masha's mom's neighbor and I guess Masha's mom has disappeared. And I'm worried...well, what if Misha ate them?

NASTYA. That shit happens.

ANNIE. Oh, my god. It does?

NASTYA. What do you wanna do about it?

ANNIE. I want to help.

NASTYA. You really want to help or just pretend that you tried?

ANNIE. I really want to help. I have to.

NASTYA. All right, I'll go get the stuff.

(NASTYA *exits.*)

ANNIE. Um, Nastya?

NASTYA. *(offstage)* What?

ANNIE. Are you really, I mean Masha said you were –

NASTYA. *(offstage)* A whore?

ANNIE. Yeah.

NASTYA. *(offstage)* Yeah.

(NASTYA *re-enters with an axe.*)

So, in *Krasnaya Shapochka* –

ANNIE. Little Red Riding Hood.

NASTYA. The woodsman uses an axe on that animal's ass.

(NASTYA *hands the axe and a black hood to* ANNIE.)

ANNIE. That's a good idea.

NASTYA. The hood will disorient him. And you'll need a pie.

ANNIE. A pie?

NASTYA. Bears are suckers for pies.

ANNIE. Okay, I'll try to pick one up.

NASTYA. Homemade is better. But do what you can do.

> *(beat)*

> What are you looking at me like that for?

ANNIE. Do you do your, uh, work *here?*

NASTYA. Yup.

> *(**ANNIE** looks down at what she's sitting on, grossed out.)*

> *Apartmenty* style. Used to do the *salon* thing with a bunch of girls. I saved for my own place.

ANNIE. Congratulations.

NASTYA. I'm getting old, you know? Twenty is thirty in whore years. I gotta be smart about making as much as I can now. So, are we done here?

ANNIE. Oh, I have to give you this. It's from Katya. She said it's only for you.

> *(**ANNIE** hands her the piece of folded paper; **NASTYA** reads it.)*

NASTYA. Katya's lost it. She's book smart, but life dumb. If I was born looking like her – she could easily work the high-end club thing. That's at least $400 a night.

> *(**NASTYA** re-enters and hands a package to **ANNIE**.)*

> I hope Katya knows what she's doing. What about you? Can you use that thing?

> *(**ANNIE** stands and lifts the axe above her head with difficulty.)*

ANNIE. *(suddenly panicked)* No, Katya will do the axe part.

NASTYA. You should know how – just in case.

ANNIE. I can't do the axe part.

NASTYA. That's natural. Just breathe deeply and remember what you're after.

ANNIE. Happily ever after?

NASTYA. Sure.

(**NASTYA** *stands behind* **ANNIE** *and helps her lift the axe.*)

Now you're going to want to brace yourself. One foot forward. Really put your weight into it. And on the count of three, we'll swing, okay? One, two –

ANNIE. Nastya?

NASTYA. What is it?

ANNIE. You're my fairy godmother.

NASTYA. There are no fairies in *skazki*.

And three.

(*They swing.*)

18. "Happily Five Minutes After."

(Lights up on NASTYA, ANNIE, *and* KATYA. ANNIE *stands in the middle with a pie plate.)*

NASTYA. *Zhili byli.*

ANNIE. Once upon a time.

KATYA. A bear lived, a bear was.

(A dim light up on the FIGURE.*)*

NASTYA. In his own little apartment at the edge of the forest. Now, this was a very bad bear.

ANNIE. Well, we don't know for sure that he's definitely bad.

KATYA. *(to* ANNIE*)* If we're going to do this, it helps to think he's bad.

ANNIE. Right.

KATYA. *Ikh zavut*

*(*KATYA *gestures to herself:)*

Katya.

*(*ANNIE *gestures nervously to herself:)*

ANNIE. *E* Anya.

They packed a pie.

NASTYA. Bears are suckers for homemade pie.

ANNIE. It's store bought. I'm never stepping foot in Yaroslava's apartment again.

NASTYA. They packed a pie.

*(*KATYA *balances the pie on her head; she slowly crouches down.)*

KATYA. Under the pie, in a big basket, they packed a girl.

NASTYA. Now, that girl had a very special surprise for the big bad bear.

KATYA. A very sharp surprise.

ANNIE. The girl in the basket was very quiet and still as she was carried –

NASTYA. – and set down at the bear's door.

(ANNIE *and* KATYA *turn to face the* FIGURE. ANNIE *knocks.*)

ANNIE. Masha? Masha, are you there? I've brought you a present.

NASTYA. The bear was curious.

ANNIE. Masha, it's only for you. Not Misha.

NASTYA. The bear was intrigued.

ANNIE. Masha, I've brought you a pie.

NASTYA. The bear was *ravenous.*

(*The* FIGURE *moves toward the pie.*)

He reached for the pie.

(*The* FIGURE *takes the pie plate.*)

ANNIE. Now for the hood.

NASTYA. Thrown over the head.

(ANNIE *puts a hood over the* FIGURE*'s head.*)

Then the girl under the pie jumped out.

KATYA. Surprise!

(KATYA *stands behind the* FIGURE *and raises the axe.* ANNIE *signals for her to wait.*)

ANNIE. Where is Masha?

NASTYA. Silly, silly grrrrls, the bear growled.

ANNIE. What did you do to her? Where is Masha's mother?

KATYA. Annichka, I've gotta do it.

ANNIE. Wait! We came to help Masha. *(to the* FIGURE*:)* Tell us where she is.

NASTYA. The bear caught a claw on the hood –

(*The* FIGURE *removes the hood.*)

Masha and her mother? He laughed.

I shred them into strips and chewed on the strings of them for hours.

Oh, they were much tougher meat than you and I gobbled them right up.

(**KATYA** *tries to swing and misses.*)

ANNIE. Throw your weight into it!

Now, Katya!

(*The* **FIGURE** *knocks the axe out of* **KATYA**'s *hand and pins her.*)

KATYA. Shit.

NASTYA. Grrrrl, the bear growled.

KATYA. *Please.*

NASTYA. I will never, ever let you go.

KATYA. *Help.*

NASTYA. The grown-up *dyevushka* knew that to really help, not just pretend that she tried...

ANNIE. Action must be taken.

(**ANNIE** *grabs the pie, throws it at the bear. The* **FIGURE** *lets go of* **KATYA**.)

Misha!

NASTYA. She dove for the axe –

ANNIE. And delivered a sharp

(*to the* **FIGURE**:)

SURPRISE!

(**ANNIE** *lifts the axe above her head and swings.*)

KATYA. Annichka!

(*The* **FIGURE** *goes down with a thud.* **KATYA** *and* **ANNIE** *stand over the body.*)

You did it.

ANNIE. What did I do? Oh my god, I killed him. I'm a killer.

KATYA. He's a bear. This is hunting, not killing. The murder comes later.

ANNIE. Nastya said a few superficial cuts to the belly should do it.

(**ANNIE** *makes a cut.*)

Oh, god. There's so much blood. I wasn't thinking about the blood.

NASTYA. And then came the magic part.

ANNIE. Something's happening.

KATYA. He's moving. Anya, hit him again!

ANNIE. Wait a second.

(*Out of the fur on the floor, an outstretched hand emerges.*)

KATYA. Oh, my god, it's –

ANNIE. Masha, hold on.

(**ANNIE** *and* **KATYA** *grab on to the hand and pull out* **MASHA**, *dressed all in red, from the fur.*)

KATYA. Masha!

(**KATYA** *and* **ANNIE** *cling to* **MASHA**.)

MASHA. Am I rescued?

KATYA. Strong-as-an-ox Annie is good with an axe.

MASHA. Annie. Something very bad could've happened to you.

ANNIE. Yeah, but – I had to take that chance.

(**MASHA** *looks down at the fur.*)

MASHA. And my mother?

NASTYA. The girls went back into the bear's belly to look for Masha's mother. But it was too late. The chewed up bits of her had already been dissolved by the acid juices in the bear's stomach. This was very sad, of course. But it also meant that Masha had now inherited two apartments and might even have some rental income to look forward to.

MASHA. Maybe I could go back to school.

ANNIE. I think that's a great idea.

NASTYA. So, the *dyevushki* lived happily for five minutes after.

KATYA. I'm so sorry, Mash, but I have to go.

MASHA. Where?

KATYA. My alibi's not going to stay blacked out forever. But this mess –

ANNIE. We can't leave it like this.

THE FAIRYTALE LIVES OF RUSSIAN GIRLS

MASHA. His family's all gone. And nobody but me's seen him for months. If we could get rid of the evidence... I don't think anybody would ever know.

ANNIE. Oh god. I know how to do it.

NASTYA. For a shot at happily ever after...

ANNIE. To make it disappear like it was never here.

(*to* **MASHA***:*) Go get cleaned up.

MASHA. What're you gonna do, Annie?

NASTYA. A *dyevushka* must walk into the iron jaws of danger.

ANNIE. Cremation.

MASHA. What?

ANNIE. In her big brick oven.

KATYA. You said you weren't going to go back in there.

ANNIE. Sometimes adults have to do things that are really effing hard.

MASHA. Annie.

ANNIE. Go get cleaned up.

Quickly.

Before there are witnesses.

(**MASHA** *nods and exits. To* **KATYA***:*)

You should go.

Before the tsar wakes up.

(**KATYA** *nods.*)

KATYA. Annie, be careful.

(**ANNIE** *nods and picks up the axe. She exits, dragging the bloody fur coat behind her.*)

NASTYA. With that, the *dyevushki* set out. Annie went in, Katya out.

(**KATYA** *places an apple on the floor and then steps back into shadows to watch as* **VALENTINA** *enters.*)

VALENTINA. Once upon a night

NASTYA. tonight

VALENTINA. is the night

NASTYA. the Other Katya studies late at Dima's

VALENTINA. and he's out God knows where

NASTYA. She knows where.

VALENTINA. Tonight

NASTYA. is the night

VALENTINA. I get the house to myself.
It's been a really fricking long time.

(VALENTINA *sees the apple. She puts a hand on her stomach, hungry.*)

Oooh, that looks good.

(*beat*)

8 medium-sized apples today at 95 calories each is...
760 calories already consumed.
Plus a number 9 is...
855.
Over 800.

NASTYA. Once upon a night...

VALENTINA. I'll treat myself anyway.

(VALENTINA *picks up the apple and takes a huge bite.*)

Oh my god, that's good.

KATYA. Midnight snack, Valentina?

VALENTINA. (*mouth full*) How did you – ?

KATYA. Pi to ten decimal places? Could a house that Katya lives in have any other code?

VALENTINA. I'm going to scream!

(KATYA *grabs her, putting a gloved hand over* VALENTINA's *mouth.* VALENTINA *starts to choke on the mouthful of apple.*)

KATYA. Just breathe and swallow, Valentina. And think about this: The fattiest thing on earth? Is the ninth apple of the day on an 800-calorie apple diet.

(VALENTINA *struggles to swallow the apple.*)

That's good, very good. Now, I just need you to do one thing for me then I swear, you will never see me again. Ever.

(**VALENTINA** *tries to fight her off.*)

All I need you to do, Valentina, is articulate know how you really feel about me.

(**VALENTINA** *pauses.*)

In writing.

(**VALENTINA** *looks at* **KATYA**.)

"Dear Katya, everything is your fault – "

(**VALENTINA** *and* **KATYA** *recede into shadows.*)

NASTYA. *Zhili byli*

ANNIE. Tonight, the oven fire…

NASTYA. …is big enough to burn a bear.

(*The fire flares as* **ANNIE** *looks on.*)

ANNIE. It's never been this large.
Or hot.

NASTYA. It was built with a thousand birch branches and two large oak logs.

ANNIE. Tonight

NASTYA. is the night

(**YAROSLAVA** *steps out. Her silhouette looks massive against the firelight.*)

YAROSLAVA. *Dyevushka!* I'm so *hungry.*

(**KATYA**, *hand still on* **VALENTINA**'s *mouth, appears.*)

KATYA. And the signature.
You've just written your own suicide note.
Addressed to your daughter.

(**KATYA** *removes her hand from* **VALENTINA**'s *mouth.*)

VALENTINA. My Katya.

(*VALENTINA goes limp;* KATYA *cushions her fall, laying her gently on the floor, a hand under her head.* KATYA *places the paper on* VALENTINA*'s chest.*)

Sleeping forever beauty.

The sweetest, loveliest thing in the world?

(*to* VALENTINA*:*)

This is my dream.

(KATYA *exits.*)

YAROSLAVA. I'm so hungry, dear, I made a great big stew.
I boiled potatoes, carrots, cabbage, beets, and onions –

ANNIE. A vegetarian stew?

(YAROSLAVA *cringes.*)

YAROSLAVA. Well, yes, I suppose at the moment it is.

ANNIE. Yaroslava Yanovna –

YAROSLAVA. Ohhhhhh, you know that's not my name, *dyevushka.*

ANNIE. Yes.

I do.

YAROSLAVA. Auntie, dear.

ANNIE. *Auntie.*

YAROSLAVA. I'm making a world-record breaking loaf of bread, but I'm not sure if the dough will fit on my gigantic bread paddle.

ANNIE. My mother didn't ask questions.

YAROSLAVA. It's a massive hunk of soft dough.

ANNIE. She just ran far, far away.

YAROSLAVA. I think it's just about the size of –

ANNIE. I could ask questions!

YAROSLAVA. The size of, well…you.

ANNIE. Would you like me to get on the paddle, *Auntie?*

(*cringe*)

So you could get an idea of how big the loaf of bread will be?

(cringe)

YAROSLAVA. Wouldn't that be nice?

ANNIE. Yes, wouldn't it?

(cringe)

How old are you, *Auntie?* Why do you look so old, *Auntie?*

YAROSLAVA. That's very impolite, dear –

ANNIE. *(overlapping)* Don't you know I'm just getting warmed up?! How did you get this apartment, *Auntie?* You took this apartment from my mother, didn't you, *Auntie?* You stole my legacy from my mother after you bit her, didn't you? What did you think you would do to *me?* Did you think you would fatten me up, then put your paws all over me, run your claws through my soft flesh? Were you planning to shred me into strips and chew on the strings of me for hours? Huh? Is that your plan? Baba Yaga? Is that what you've been doing to girls for years, Baba Yaga?

*(**YAROSLAVA** cowers, convulsing with pain. In the meantime, **ANNIE** has picked up the nearby axe and holds it up over her head.)*

YAROSLAVA. Stop!

Please.

ANNIE. Why should I?

(cringe)

YAROSLAVA. *Dyevushka,* all I've ever tried to do is feed you. You wouldn't hurt an old lady who looks like she might be a *babushka* begging on the Moscow metro.

ANNIE. You don't know what I can do.

*(**YAROSLAVA** breathes a breath of relief – not a question! – and advances on **ANNIE**.)*

YAROSLAVA. Oh, but I *do,* darling. After all, you are one-half Olga.

ANNIE. She told me to reap my rewards.

YAROSLAVA. But what did she do herself? She promised you to me.

ANNIE. My mom left the apartment to save me.

YAROSLAVA. Then why did she send you back?

ANNIE. She said –

YAROSLAVA. She sent you right back to me.

ANNIE. – business opportunities.

YAROSLAVA. All these years in a land far, far away, living not quite happily ever after? She began to think she'd made the wrong choice.

ANNIE. No.

YAROSLAVA. *Yes.*

ANNIE. No.

YAROSLAVA. My little orphan.

You're not a killer.

ANNIE. I don't know.

YAROSLAVA. You're not.

You're just a little girl

You don't need to be an adult, dear.

(*A beat.* ANNIE *drops the axe.*)

Good girl.

Idi sooda.

(ANNIE *steps toward her.* YAROSLAVA *puts out her arms.* ANNIE *steps into* YAROSLAVA*'s arms.*)

My sweet little niece.

ANNIE. Auntie.

(YAROSLAVA *sniffs* ANNIE*'s hair.*)

YAROSLAVA. So juicy.

ANNIE. My bones.

YAROSLAVA. Like freshly-baked bread.

And stew.

The smell of the Rus is so strong in you.

ANNIE. But I'm also part American citizen.

YAROSLAVA. Oh, I'll just bite that bit out.

(**YAROSLAVA** *lunges for* **ANNIE**'s *heart, jaws wide open.*
NASTYA, **KATYA**, *and* **MASHA** *return.*)

NASTYA. *Zhili byli.*

(*The metallic sound of* **YAROSLAVA**'s *teeth.*)

MASHA. Baba Yaga.

KATYA. Must be cooked

ANNIE. In her own oven.

(**ANNIE** *pushes* **YAROSLAVA** *into the fire.*)

NASTYA. Two suicides in one night. An oligarch's wife leaves a not-so-nice note behind for her daughter. And an old-lady recluse sticks her head in the oven. Very sad, of course, but this shit happens.

ANNIE. *(to* **NASTYA***)* My fairy godmother.

MASHA. We have to clean up this mess.

ANNIE. I'll start with the gigantic broom.

MASHA. You'll do no such thing.

KATYA. You need to run far, far away.

ANNIE. *Dyevushki.*

MASHA. Quickly.

Before there are witnesses.

ANNIE. I want to stay and reap my rewards. I've earned it.

KATYA. You need to go.

MASHA. You did the same for me.

(*A beat. To* **NASTYA***:*)

ANNIE. Then take the apartment.

NASTYA. Are you serious?

ANNIE. You might have some rental income to look forward to.

(**NASTYA** *smiles.*)

NASTYA. Improbably, impossibly.

There can be happily ever afters.

ANNIE. Now I have my own *skazka* to tell.

KATYA. A few weeks pass. Thing settle down, daughters burn nasty last letters. And soon the happiest *dyevushka* in the whole wide world has a tsar for a husband *and* a father.

(NASTYA *takes off her wig to become the* OTHER KATYA. KATYA *addresses her:*)

I'll be the very best mother and sister there ever was. I'm sorry I wasn't honest with you from the very beginning.

(OTHER KATYA *crosses to her.*)

MASHA. A few weeks pass. Things settle down. And still – no one seems to notice that once upon a night...

KATYA. Annie the American disappeared.

OTHER KATYA. Home to sunny California?

MASHA. I sure as hell hope so.

KATYA. Nothing was left behind.

Just a brick oven full of ashes,

the world's largest vegetarian stew gone cold,

and an old fur coat with a hole shaped like the Soviet Union.

There was no sign that Anya Rabinovich had ever stepped foot in apartment 57.

(*A wonderful thing:*)

MASHA. She ran far, far away and disappeared like she was never here.

OTHER KATYA. The end.

(*Lights down. The end.*)

CPSIA information can be obtained
at www.ICGtesting.com
Printed in the USA
LVHW081827310520
657067LV00022B/2978